The Crinkling on a Poisonous Pie

A Fable

Phillip Leighton-Daly

Ordering Information:

Prime Seven Media
518 Landmann St.
Tomah City, WI 54660

Printed in the United States of America

The Crinkling on a Poisonous Pie

This title was inspired by William King from a rhyming couplet penned in his The Art of Cookery published in 1708.

Unless some sweetness at the bottom lie.
Who cares for all the crinkling of the pie.

Readers in this story are challenged to ascertain the value of wealth, beauty and youthfulness in the absence of empathy and compassion.

Other Books by the Author

- <u>Recollections of the Central Coast NSW</u> – 2004 – Goulburn. ISBN 646– 444252.

- Reflective History of the Goulburn District Volume I. – <u>Life's Hard School</u> – 2010. Goulburn. ISBN 9780980809305.

- Reflective History of the Goulburn District Volume II. – <u>Taking a Chance</u> – 2010.Goulburn. ISBN 97809809312.

- A Reflective History of the Goulburn District Volume III.– <u>But of the Hut I Built</u>. – 2010. Goulburn. ISBN 9780980809329.

- A Reflective History of the Goulburn District Volume IV – <u>The Tides and the Lives of Men.</u> 2016.Goulburn. ISBN 9780980809343.

- This book won the 2015 Goulburn – Mulwaree Heritage Award for historical research. "Preserving Goulburn – Mulwaree's Heritage."

- A Reflective History of the Goulburn District Volume V – <u>Wrinkled Armpits and Woollybutts</u> – The Past and Present Significance of Native Flora in the Goulburn District, 2017. Goulburn. ISBN 9780980809350.

- Kenmore Psychiatric Hospital Volume I. Wednesday's Child. – 2014. Goulburn. This book won the 2014 Goulburn – Mulwaree Heritage Award for historical research.
- Recollections of Wider Goulburn – <u>Hither, Thither and Yon</u>. 2018, 9780980809367.
- Reflections of the Goulburn District. <u>The Towrang Stockade</u>. Goulburn. 2018. 9780980808381.

Juvenile Adult Fiction

The Prince who Wanted to Live Forever.
The Fisherman and his Foundlings.
Elizabeth's Garden. Honorable Thieves.
The Crinkling on the Pie. No Honor Among Thieves.
The Boiling Toad. The Feral Menace.
Rowing Against the Tide.

Table of Contents

Colonization in Space

In the year 2080 AD, probes were launched from the planet Earth. Two distant planets orbiting a sun were adjudged suitable for colonization. Just as the Quakers and Pilgrims established colonies in the New World, an ancient Galilean sect established colonies on the planets.

These 21st century pilgrims were disciples of Chrystos, the teacher crucified by the Roman governor Pontius Pilate. Clinging tenaciously to 2000 - year old traditions, they stoically resisted the pressures imposed by the early church. Traditional occupations such as carpenters, fishermen and sheepherders were valued and retained by the sect. The Galileans earnestly sought to establish a new world order free from prejudice and hatred.

But even during the first fifty years of settlement, frightening transformations were taking place. Here in lies a report of those distressing times.

An asteroid belt lay between the planets of Greyce and Kaire.

Life on Greyce

The newly colonized planets were richly endowed with natural resources. Gold, silver, iron, uranium, and coal presented many trade opportunities throughout the solar system. Immediately the Greycians chose to adjust their religious beliefs in accord with their newly acquired wealth.

As a consequence of increased wealth, power and pleasure, the Greycians empathized Christos's sacrifice on the cross. "We are all sinners and we are all forgiven," they boasted. The magnitude of their indiscretions seemed to be of little consequence. The basis for this decision lay in their holy book's scripture, "Believe in Christos, and you and your family will be saved."[1]

Christos's name became all important, his ministry even lesser so. Failure to worship him resulted in the most horrible punishments.

---

[1]   Acts Chapter 16, Verse 31. p.146. Holy Bible – NSW Revised Standard Version, 1989, Division of Christian Education of the National Council of the Churches of Christ in the USA.

This had occurred earlier on Earth where non- believers in Christos were sentenced to death or eternal damnation. Though the Greycians worshipped Christos as a God, their behavior grew increasingly selfish and cruel. This was a stark contravention of his message, namely caring and forgiveness.

Christos's charity and good works were soon relegated by the Greycians and deemed unimportant. A Goolag (labor camp) was established on the asteroid belt where those failing to exalt Christos were incarcerated. Rarely were they seen again.

The Greycians felt no compulsion to model themselves on Christ.
They were forgiven and would continue to be forgiven,
no matter the atrocity. His sacrifice on the cross ensured that.

The lives of the Greycians increasingly revolved around pleasure, wealth, and power. Though horrible atrocities such as assassinations were regularly committed, all guilt was quickly absolved through confession. "Christos died for us and we are forgiven."

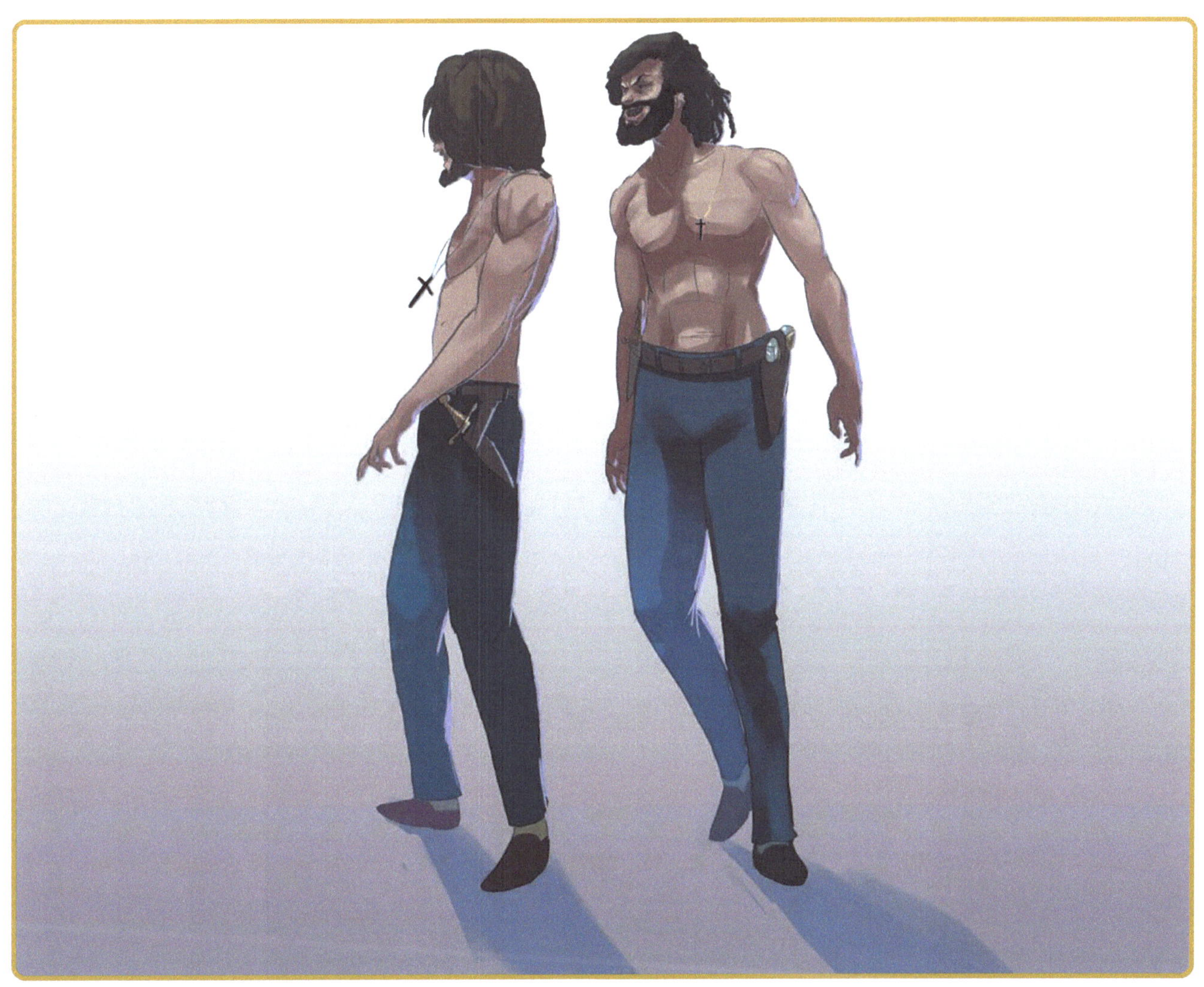

Criminals on Greyce enjoyed a free rein. Drug peddlers, extortionists, and murderers proudly displayed golden crucifixes and tattoos, signifying their belief in Christos. "We donate generously to the church. Christos is Lord, Hallelujah!"

For Greycians, physical appearance soon became of primary importance. Tall, powerful boys and tall, slender girls were adjudged racially superior. Cloning and in vitro fertilization were common place; steroid use widespread. Beauty and youthfulness became clearly more important than one's deeds. Beauty often equated to power, wealth and pleasure. Intelligence and morality became irrelevant.

The diseased and decrepit suffered much rejection on Greyce. Most were marooned in ghettos on the asteroid belt.

Arrogant and conceited, Greycian athletes basked in self‑ adoration, their festive-filled days distorted by legal and illegal drugs. Fair-weather groupies worshipped them. As badges of honor, the athletes prominently displayed their medals.

Selfishness along with the affluent lifestyles, drugs, and cosmetic surgery, ensured that vitality and radiance were retained into old age.

This budding religion, modelled upon and dedicated to Christos bore little resemblance to his ministry.

Physical appearances grew increasingly popular on Greyce.

The Anointed One

The Anointed One, a self-proclaimed prophet and the leader of Greyce, bestowed pretentious and grandiose titles upon himself. As a preacher, his style was unparalleled. His sermons began and ended in a spectacular fashion. He descended from heaven on a tightrope. He dressed in weird costumes. Parishioners were introduced to a range of biblical characters like the shepherd, David, whirling his sling above his head,

to the beautiful and vengeful Salome, with the
head of John the Baptist on a platter,

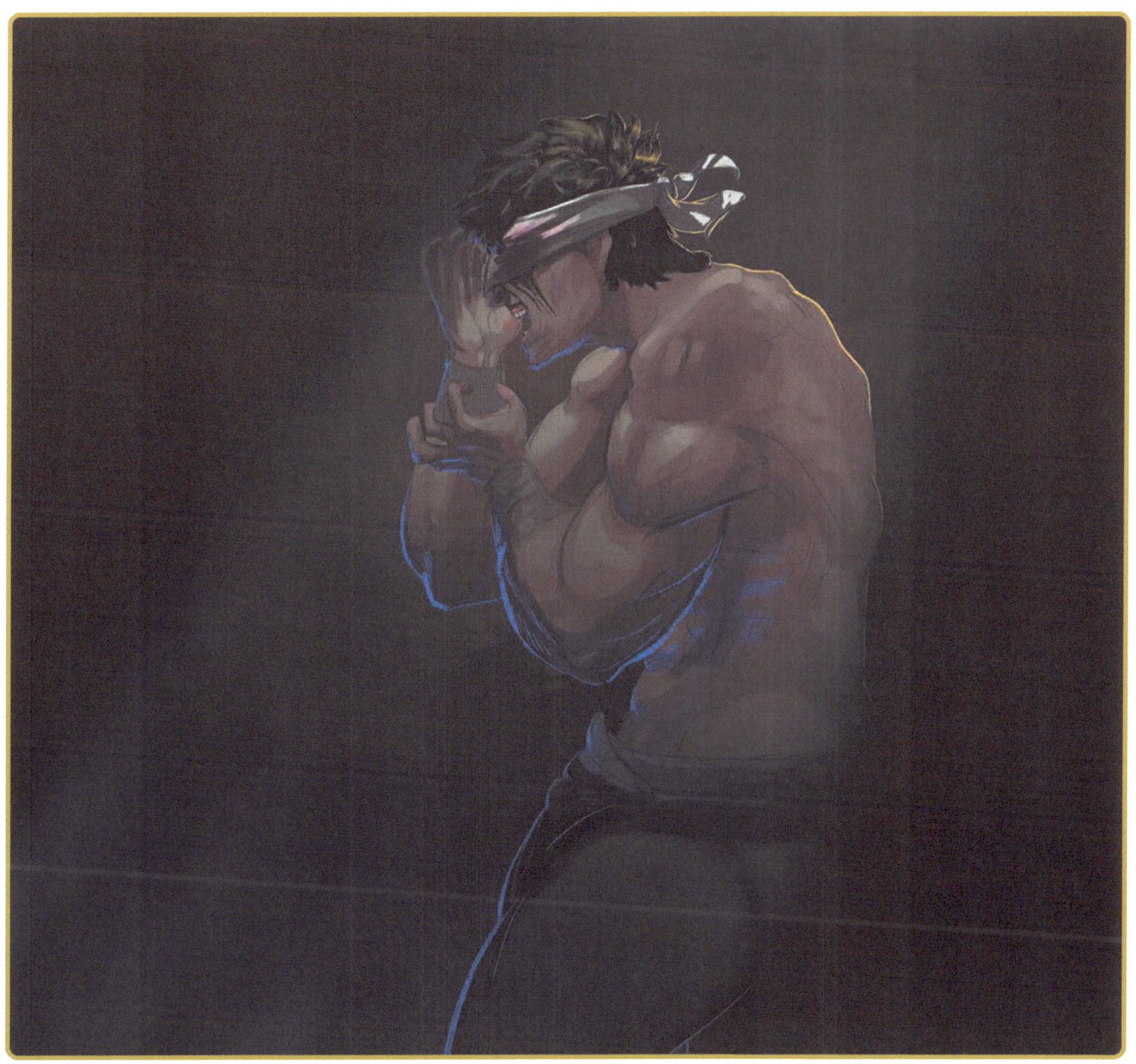

to Sampson, with his eyes gouged out and his hair cropped.

to Jude, the brother of Christos who was
crucified and used for target practice,

to Peter who was crucified upside down,

and to Daniel in the lions' den.

The Anointed One frequently paraded as archangels, the highest order of angels. He identified strongly with Michael, the warrior archangel who championed mercy, justice and righteousness. Jophiel, the archangel of Beauty, and Gabriel the Messenger were also held in high regard.

Raphael, the Archangel of Healing, and Michael, the
Archangel of Mercy, frequently accompanied the Anointed
One, pirouetting occasionally in majestic splendor.

His Most Glorified Majesty ended his performances with the same exuberance with which he began; he ascended to heaven on a tightrope. The parishioners always responded with a raucous, standing ovation. Such was their leader's popularity that live telecasts of his sermons were transmitted around the galaxy.

The charismatic preacher was the fountain from which all manner of emotion spouted. Tears of joy, grief, or gratitude were instantly manifest. Spectacular backflips and cartwheels appeared authentic enough, but alas, in that respect his parishioners were deceived. The preacher's twin brother, a champion gymnast, performed these acrobatic feats shrouded in a misty purple haze. No one doubted the preacher's authenticity though, "It's the divine intervention of God," they declared.

Selecting Suitable Scriptures

The Anointed One preached select scriptures relevant to his debased lifestyle. Sacred texts relating to wealth and adultery, were conveniently overlooked while others such as man's dominion over all beasts were embraced.[2] Responding to the license to indiscriminately kill animals, the parishioners quickly hunted all the planet's rich and diverse wildlife into extinction. It was not only scriptures that The Anointed One chose to misrepresent. Ariel, the Archangel of Nature and Animals was largely ignored. Ariel had been entrusted with the rejuvenation and protection of the planet's resources.

---

[2]   Genesis Chapter 1. Verse 28. p.2. "And God blessed them, and said unto them, be fruitful, and multiply, and fill the earth, and subdue it: and have dominion over the fish of the sea, and over the fowl of the air, and over every living thing that moves upon the earth." Holy Bible – NSW Revised Standard Version, 1989, Division of Christian Education of the National Council of the Churches of Christ in the USA.

This misguided leadership led to the adoption of game hunting as a national sport. The family ownership of firearms became mandatory. Towering steel cages were constructed on the land and from the ocean beds. From these refuges, hunters waited in deadly ambush, eliminating all lifeforms, large or small. Savage mammals such as hippopotami, elephants and giraffes were favored. For slaughtering a lioness and her cub, or a whale with calf, marksmen received golden medallions.

This was known as the 'daily double'. Parishioners warmed to photographs of hunters standing over their kill. The Photographer of the Year award featured a marksman holding the remains of a frog shot from a distance of 100 metres!

In the execution towers, or Exec Towers as they were popularly known, these intrepid hunters received special privileges. Alluring waitresses attended to the hunters' every whim. Refreshments, alcohol, narcotics, movies and even massages were available.

Limitations were initially imposed upon the consumption of alcohol and narcotics. Drug affected shooters tended to demolish towers and buildings with their highly powered rocketry. Exemptions were forthcoming of course for the Anointed One and his inner sanctum. Concessions were also given to friends, family members or those offering inducements of money or favors.

Restrictions were also imposed on the use of explosive weaponry such as napalm and land mines. Though deaths from such misfortunes were everyday events, it soon became apparent that denial of their use was a violation of the Prime Amendment. Compelling arguments regarding human rights soon resulted in the withdrawal of all limitations. Rocketry was popular for it allowed even the most inaccurate hunters to record kills. These detonations destroyed all life within five square metres.

As the numbers of animals dwindled, the Anointed One paraded strongly for the import of wildlife from other planets. The powerful gun lobby supported him strongly, arguing "What use is game hunting as a national sport if we have hunted all the animals into extinction!"

Despite the absurdity of the argument, the flora and fauna on Greyce was replenished with wildlife from around the solar system. Feral pests such as foxes, rabbits, feral cats and dogs, water buffalo and cane toads were readily obtainable and inexpensive. These pests quickly over-ran the land; carp, crown of thorn star fish and red fin infested their waterways. Few complaints were received from the hunters. The national sport had been reinvigorated and all parishioners were now free to resume their whole hearted, indiscriminate slaughter.

Prior to the replenishment of animals on Greyce, the Anointed One mounted an unprecedented attack on Ariel, the Archangel of Nature and Animals. "Ariel, is a lay about"; he claimed, "He has forsaken our planet." One could readily imagine how such disrespect might result in some unfortunate consequence, that some dreadful judgement might be wrought upon the parishioners of Greyce.

There was of course, a terrible down side to this national past-time and the Prime Amendment. Unhinged and revolutionary Greycians often turned their weaponry upon the parishioners. Horrendous death counts were incurred.

To the mass killings, The Anointed One's response was immediate and anticipated. It was almost as though he had welcomed such atrocities. His memorial services were televised widely and much wealth flowed into his personal coffers.

These staged memorial services bore a strong resemblance to pro-wrestling on the planet Earth. The Anointed One appeared as the Archangel of Death, Azrael.

Sullen, dour and forlorn, he dressed in pale loose-fitting garments. He greeted the large gathering thus. "Brethren, truly a tragedy of the highest order. Most unfortunate though unavoidable." He emphasized 'unavoidable' for ownership of weaponry was sacrosanct and no interference with its use would be tolerated.

On mention of the phrase "most unfortunate though unavoidable", the Anointed One commenced his grand performance. His face contorted dreadfully as if he had suffered a stroke. His bottom lip drooped and began to tremble. He began to drool and tears streamed down his cheeks. The parishioners sat spellbound. Then he began to babble incoherently as if summoning a spirit from the underworld. He had of course commenced a five-minute discourse in tongues. "Oh bac or sor cot rammo ... The only difference here to the biblical version was that no-one had the faintest notion of what he was gibbering about. This nonsensical gabble continued until interrupted by several winged creatures fluttering onto the scene. The parishioners recognized them immediately as Raphael, the Archangel of Healing, Michael, the Archangel of Mercy and Chamuel, the Archangel of Peace. These heavenly personages circled the Anointed One, pirouetting occasionally in majestic splendor. After an eruption of purple smoke, they disappeared.

These performances were immensely popular; the solemnity of the situation was either forgotten or adjudged irrelevant to all, except the mourners who had suffered great loss. A low value was placed on human life on Greyce.

The Anointed One was adjudged leader of the colony for reasons other than his ministry. His wealth exceeded that of all other parishioners. He owned castles surrounded by moats, shuttle craft and even submarines. A plethora of academic and achievement awards were festooned throughout the church. Most were purchased or acquired through favours and gifts.

Though the Anointed One's life was a direct contravention of the teachings of Christos, he believed that his unwavering acceptance of one scripture, assured him eternal life.

The Anointed One's selective appropriation of scripture resulted in conflict and suffering on Greyce, just as it had defiled the Christian faith on Earth. Never once did the Anointed One ever encourage his parishioners to turn away from their evil.[3]

---

[3]   Ephesians Chapter 5. Verse 15. Holy Bible – NSW Revised Standard Version, 1989, Division of Christian Education of the National Council of the Churches of Christ in the USA.

Life on Kaire

Unlike their capitalistic neighbors, parishioners from the planet Kaire, focused upon welfare work for the sick and downtrodden. "Man is remembered," they believed, "for what he gives to the world, rather than what he takes from it."[4] Their life was essentially an existence spent assisting others. Creed, color, race and status were never determining factors.

Parishioners on Kaire radiated an inner glow; their faces were etched with compassion. They clung to a plethora of scriptures such as "Blessed are those who are generous because they feed the poor."[5]

Like their neighbors, the Kairians believed in the forgiveness of sins, but earnestly sought to better their lives and become more like Christos. Heaven for parishioners on Kaire, did not involve material rewards in the

---

[4]   Reflecting upon the philosophy of Morris Fishdean.

[5]   Proverbs. Chapter 22. Verse 9. p. 632. Holy Bible – NSW Revised Standard Version, 1989, Division of Christian Education of the National Council of the Churches of Christ in the USA.

afterlife. Paradise was an exalted state attained throughout their life on the planet. This was obtained through adherence to the teachings of Christos and the inner peace drawn from a life lived for others.

Infirmity, disease and death was more readily accepted than those from their neighboring planet. Kairians identified strongly with Christos, his selfless ministry and his sacrifice. They staunchly comforted the sick and grieving during their many trials. Faith healing was very real and suffering was seen as the building blocks of character.

Though prayer and reverence were adjudged sacrosanct, long hours of worshipping Christos or his father was seen as wasteful, a primitive custom practised in pagan times on Earth. Righteousness and selflessness were the standards that the people deemed important.

On Kaire, valuable medical discoveries were made. The extraction of properties from the planet's abundant flora and fauna gave rise to valuable pharmaceutical discoveries. From the flightless Dodo, a cure for epilepsy was discovered, from the Stellers Sea Cow, a cure for skin complaints, and from the Tasmanian Tiger, a cure for cancer.

Antibiotic properties found in a grass fern and daisy mountain bush averted much suffering and death. All such plants and animals were extinct both on Greyce and on Mother Earth.

Valuable medical ingredients were extracted from
the Dodo and Tasmanian Tiger. On Earth and Greyce
these animals were hunted into extinction.

Athletes on Kaire saw their gifts as transient. They thus found it essential to promote and inspire the handicapped, lesser endowed, and younger members of their society.

For those from the planet Greyce who were preoccupied with size and muscular development, it was a bitter pill for them to witness the superhuman feats of those from Kaire. Sherpa-type individuals half their size, lumbered heavy weights to high, rarefied mountain peaks. And small framed warriors defeated their larger counterparts in martial arts competitions.

Over time, the physiological traits of those on Kaire and Greyce evolved noticeably. Growth in empathy on Kaire had intensified, owing to the caring nature of their lives. Heart disease plummeted due to the contentment they received from their fulfilling welfare work and their ground breaking medical discoveries.

Little intellectual growth was evident on Greyce over the same period. Their focus on physical appearance was apparent.

Visitors from Kaire looked upon their neighbors as 'shallow'; those on Greyce regarded theirs as 'boorish.'

Sherpas on the planet Kaire, could handle twice the loads in treacherous mountain terrain than the top athletes from Greyce.

33

Interplanetary Rivalries

Though the Galileans shared common values on colonization, cracks began to appear in their relationship. The Greycians argued that Christos was God, that God, Christos and the Holy Spirit were one.

The Kairians refused to argue about such matters. Such information had been decided by bishops on Earth. They were intent on securing authority and control. Scores of malicious arguments (schisms) had resulted in the ratification of contentious issues such as the Trinity on Earth. The Kairians focused primarily on humanitarian issues and in adopting a Christos like persona.

The delivery of provisions by the Kairians to the refugees on the asteroid belt caused resentment.

Disrespect by Greycians towards senior citizens was another bone of contention. The guidance and wisdom provided by senior citizens was an integral feature in governance on Kaire.

Surely the greatest bone of contention was one of belief. The Kairians professed caring, forgiveness and love. These were the models proposed by Christos.

The Greycians believed that overt declarations of faith whether sincere or not, were essential in obtaining eternal life.

In the eyes of the Kairians, many of those imprisoned or exiled on the asteroid belt were being unfairly punished for their humanitarian services. Rescue parties relocated them to Kaire. Skirmishes broke out and lives were lost.

Harsh words were exchanged between the now two distinct sects. The Kairians accused their neighbors of misrepresenting Christos and ignoring his ministry. The Greycians claimed that in failing to glorify Christos, the pleasures of the afterlife would be denied them.

The Invasion of Greyce and Kaire

Ominous black clouds were gathering. A dangerous, militant civilization scanned the planets with interest. Envoys were dispatched with devious intentions of colonizing them.

These deputations first appeared on Greyce in forms appealing to the parishioners' vanity. The Anointed One was quickly seduced by glamourous envoys. He greeted his visitors resplendently attired and remarked how timely his recent chin tuck and nose job had been. After cordial discussions, with his arms draped affectionately around his female consorts, he entered their shuttlecraft. No one saw him again.

One by one, all parishioners from Greyce were lured aboard that shuttle through flattery or the promise of great wealth. Men and women were quickly deceived by beautiful young maidens and handsome adonizes.

After one month, all the parishioners had vanished, and the colonization was complete. The whereabouts of the Greycians remained a great mystery.

The Anointed One greeted the aliens affectionately. "How timely my recent chin tuck and nose job had been," he declared.

On Kaire, the aliens attempted various deceptions, all with no success. The telepathic abilities of the elderly citizens saw through the guise and no parishioners were ever lured aboard the aliens' shuttlecraft.

Assuredly, the aliens had the military power to quickly subdue all life on Kaire. But the inhabitants' superior intellectual and empathetic powers along with their valuable medical break-throughs were held in high regard. Man's appearance was valued far less important to his utility or usefulness to his fellow man. An alliance was forged between them.

The Stagnant Pond

One year after the Great Alliance was consecrated, the aliens organized educational tours to the great asteroid belt. This spectacular array of rocky fragments lay between the planets of Kaire and Greyce. The most mystifying of all exhibits was The Stagnant Pond.

A delegation of elders from Kaire were invited to the grand opening. Never in their wildest imaginings could they have prepared themselves for such a shock!

First impressions of the asteroid were in accord with the tourist brochure, The Stagnant Pond. The surrounding ocean was totally awash with plastic waste. Mining excavations had disfigured the landscape; they appeared as a series of unsightly, festering wounds, infected by discolored pools of poisonous discharge. Atomic detonations had rendered some districts inhabitable. Dams and creeks were infested with rich blooms of blue green algae. Dogs, sheep and cattle lay dead and dying from the algae's insidious poison.

But further afield the scenery changed noticeably; a most picturesque city, richly adorned by multi-storied buildings loomed on the horizon. Foremost of these magnificent structures was a most beautiful cathedral. "Why is such a beautiful creation seen as stagnant?" inquired a female church elder from Kaire. The alien chose not to answer her.

There before the Kairians towered the cathedral in all its magnificence, its ivory towers, cedar furnishings, and stained- glass windows. It was a replica of the cathedral on Greyce. The foyer was festooned with beautiful tapestries. Golden messages were inscribed on them, such as 'Saved by Grace'.

The entire colony was seated inside the church. As a shroud, a deathly silence hung over that congregation. The Anointed One hung balanced above the throng on a tightrope. He was dressed on this occasion as Sampson, the strongman. His eyes were affixed on six attractive women in the front pew. They were obviously as captivated by his daring, as he was by their beauty. They smiled alluringly and their arms were raised as if waving. They greeted his gaze unashamedly despite the presence of the Anointed One's wife, who sat behind them. She too sat fixated on her husband's daring. On her left, her three young children sat mesmerized, and to her right sat her partner. He had one arm cozily draped around her and she hers around him. All knew him as her toy boy. Both looked a picture of health personified. She, in particular appeared so stunning and invigorated, the Belle of the Ball. How timely her recent facelift, liposuction and silicone implants had proven to be.

All the colony of Greyce were present in the congregation, and all looked amazingly youthful. It was plainly a Sunday service; the parishioners had expectantly gathered for one primary reason. The Anointed One would surely absolve them of their terrible transgressions from the previous week.

But something was horribly amiss. No one in the congregation moved. All looked amazingly lifelike though frozen in time, like wax models in a museum.

At this point, the aliens chose to reveal themselves in their true form. Large, pebbly, toad-like creatures stood crouched and crippled before the elders from Kaire. Each was horribly disfigured by radiation.

And suddenly, it became apparent to the delegation why their colony had not suffered a fate similar to Greyce. Their telepathic intelligence, empathy, compassion and medical achievements had far greater utility than the vanity of their neighbors.

The selfish quest for power, wealth, pleasure and eternal life had led to the sudden and absolute destruction of the colony known as Greyce.

The Aftermath

Millions of tourists flooded to the Stagnant Pond attraction. It became the most popular drawcard in the cosmos. The once adorned, most beautiful tapestry, soon hung forlornly as a soiled and decrepit piece of cloth. Surely there is no grace given for those wallowing in wickedness.

Biography

Phil has compiled 10 local non-fiction books over ten years. Wednesday's Child, is the most widely known and has been circulated throughout numerous libraries throughout the world.

Ten of Phil's short stories (3000 word fiction) have been self-published. Three of these have been revised to 1400 words, and await publication.

Until the onset of Covid, Phil worked for the NSW Education Department. Much of his 45 years' service has been in one and two - teacher schools. Here he has taught his 2 children for their entire infants and primary education (Kindergarten to Year 6).

Phil has taught throughout NSW, on the coast, tablelands, western slopes and plains. He has taught in one teacher, central, mainstream and a specialist school which catered for physically and mentally challenged students. For over ten years he has also instructed students in water safety and survival swimming for the NSW Education and Sport and Recreation departments.

Phil has interests in most outdoor sports. He plays competitive tennis, kayaks, swims, and bushwalks around the wilds of Bungonia Gorge. It is from his incursions into these desolate and rugged wildernesses that the genesis for many of his adventures have been drawn.

He enjoys karaoke and sings in the Sing Australia Choir. Phil also assists the needy and infirm at a small local church.

Married for over 40 years, he has two children and a loyal Lurcher rescue dog named Marley.

Phil's parents served in World War II, his dad in New Guinea and his mum as a nurse at war hospitals in Sydney and at Kenmore near Goulburn, NSW.

Phil has diplomas in General Primary Teaching and Bible Studies. He has been the proud recipient of 6 Bronze Medallions (Life Saving awards) and a 25 – year Austswim service certificate.